CU01085102

RIGᴇᴌ

THE BOY WHO
BECAME A FAIRY

Volume 1:

A Mysterious Planet

A fantasy novel by

DeLiang Al-Farabi (8 years old)

RIGEL – Volume 1: A Mysterious Planet

Written by **DeLiang Al-Farabi**

Editor: **Stephen**

Cover and Layouting by **@aira.rumi**

@2020 DeLiang AL-Farabi

Published by **NEA Publishing**

MEET THE AUTHOR

Muhammad DeLiang Al-Farabi was born in Taipei, Taiwan 18 June 2012.

He grew up in Bristol, England after spending his early childhood in Indonesia.

When he was 7 years old, he published three illustrating books for the toddler. This novel is his first four novels that launched at the same time.

CONTENTS

PROLOGUE

Once there was a humble family with a young eight-year-old boy. He was smart, but sometimes he could be a bit incautious.

His appearance was not like other humans. Something hidden inside shone in his transcendent features.

Things were quite normal until a single bizarre event changed his whole life ...

What is it?

He encounters an unimaginable world in a mysterious forest where he finds a fantastic planet.

He has to fight iniquitous, dangerous monsters who want to destroy the peaceful, amiable world in that mysterious place.

But how can he help this unearthly planet?

Time is running out.

The hero finds that not only is the planet magical, but it is also cyclopean, the size of the biggest star!

He needs some friends to help him, but what sort? Powerful or useless? Friendly or evil? Smart or dumb?

There are millions of vicious monsters: the only way to complete his mission is to destroy all of them.

Things start to get worse and worse each time before the hero meets this smart, wicked enemy.

So how does he protect the planet?

It all starts one summer day when he was playing in the joyful sunlight ...

CHAPTER 1

In a country somewhere in the northwest quadrant of earth, out in the countryside, a humble family lived in a tiny, shabby house passed down by generations. The family now consisted of a lazy, beautiful older sister, a weird-looking boy, a protective, intelligent mother, and a healthy, true-hearted father.

One day, the family went outside to play in the mesmerising sunshine. The boy, whose name was Rigel, was running, laughing with delight. The family had not seen the sun in months.

One hour later...

While they were all playing joyfully, the boy suddenly heard a thundery noise followed by weird gurgles. The charming sky turned to darkness -- filled with countless turquoise lights hitting the ground in less than a millisecond.

The family saw a Brobdingnagian forest starting to rise into the (sky filled with) darkness. They were horror-struck to see red glowing eyes glaring at them (in the forest). But the red eyes were not like any normal eyes, as they had encountered before. They were more monstrous than anything they had ever experienced in their quiet lives. Everyone went mad. Chaos…

RUMMMMBBLE!

Bit by bit, the massive, mysterious forest started to cover the peaceful countryside. But the worst part was the creatures were jumping out of this all-conquering forest.

Countless monsters of four different types began unexpectedly appearing out of thin air. The way they looked could send shivers down your spine and make you faint.

One monster had a hexagonal pyramid-shaped head almost completely filled with one evil eye. It had a frowning mouth, a purplish-dark face that could dazzle your eyes, a two-meter black hole as a body streaked with some vomit-brown colour, and snake-legs with red-purple patterns. It also had grey bomb-feet and poisonous arms with 2.5-m claws. The feet could explode and grow back in a matter of seconds.

The second monster was not as scary as the first, but it could still make you retreat to safety. It had about 200 dark-peach-coloured eyes, a hypnotiser as a nose, and a ten-metre hammer on both of his hairy, slippery arms. The arms and hands' colour was pale purple, but the hammer was some mysterious black. However, the scariest thing was that he was half the size of the entire forest – without any visible leg/s! The body was bloodcurdling red.

The third monster had a flower-shaped head. It was dark purple all over. The eyes were located on each of the ten petals they had, and it had a circle mouth filled with 120 rows of teeth covering its entire mouth.

This monster's arms had their own 12 rows of teeth at the edge of its hands! The hands' devil colour was pale red, and these hands had white pulsing veins, the monster's body was thick, about 30 meters wide. The colour of this monster's body was dark brown, and her legs were like real-life ghosts!

But all these monsters were nothing compared to the fourth monster. This monster was also half the size of the forest, yet the monster only had a head, two legs, and two arms. Her head included a mouth with thousands rows of teeth and two poisonous snake-like tongues. The colour of this monster's face was strangely black, and the twin tongues' colour was a pale purple. This monster had eyes with thin pupils but no eyebrows. Her arms could spit out lava all over the place, and her feet were ever so sharp, like a dagger. The colour of both the arms and legs was devilish red.

Those monsters surrounded the family in the middle of a slow-forming circle. The family was begging the monsters not to attack them.

Suddenly, a mysterious vigorous force sent the family flying into the countless creatures – but somehow only the mother and father felt the full effect of the force. The parents immediately shouted to their half confused, half-frightened children:

'CHILDREN ... RUN AS FAST AS YOU CAN! SAVE YOURSELVES!!!!!!!'

Rigel and his sister realised what they had to do, so they ran faster than a speeding car, trying to get to the way out. However, the supersonic forest rose before they reached the path. Rigel looked back at his parents, but they had already vanished. The boy had no choice but to run into the creepy forest with his sister.

But as he was about to enter the forest, the boy was suddenly blocked by one of the second types of monsters trying to attack him. He was being hypnotised by the creature's 'hypnotiser nose' from which blazed a shining light which was slowly starting to control his body.

However, the boy was smart enough to come up with a quick plan: he took out a pair of dark sunglasses and put them on, shielding his eyes. He had put the sunglasses in his pocket before he went out to play as the sun had been shining so brightly.

'These dark sunglasses protect my eyes from the hypnotiser, and the sunglasses will reflect the light at the monster, and he will soon be still' the boy thought with a grin.

And sure enough, the plan worked. Soon, the monster was still as a statue. Only his eyes were moving around crazily, like trying to tell a message to the boy. The boy was lucky there were no more monsters behind the big one. So he walked into the forest. But he soon realised that his sister had disappeared, too.

He then carefully walked more and more quickly into the forest, panicking. He saw not one single monster in the forest, none. He only saw people sleeping on luxurious beds. On one of the beds lay his mother, father, and sister. It was deathly quiet; it was so quiet that he only heard people snoring. He also heard his heart beating fast.

His heart was thumping faster and faster when a *CLASH* sound broke the silence. Rigel was curious where the sound could have come from; so, he walked further and further into the silent forest. Suddenly, a sparkling path appeared out of thin air where people were flying and fighting with powers.

***

The boy walked through the entrance. He was amazed. But before he knew it, he started to fly. He immediately realised that he was hovering above the 'magic' world. All around, the boy saw sparkling, bright houses and people.

On one side, there was a place that looked as if something — probably a small asteroid -- had burned it. A sign covered it:

DON)T G&O IN' SI.DE (TRANS: don't go inside)

The boy saw the people fighting -- but harmlessly, though.

One of the people was using a well-known power, superhuman strength. She stopped a giant house when she was attacked. Everyone froze.

Some other people became interested in the boy. They started to stare at Rigel with such great curiosity that they almost did not blink.

To the people staring at him, Rigel looked handsomely hypnotising with an oval-shaped head which is uncommon in the magic world, 1.5 m tall, striking eyes with large, green irises, a bent nose, scruffy hair, and triangular ears. What they did not know was he had seven toes in his left foot covered by his ripped black shoes.

The incomprehensible people started to mutter about Rigel. They all had pointed ears, but each had a differently shaped head. One had a parallelogram shape, and another had a pentagon shaped-head. They had muscular, oval, or thin body shapes.

Suddenly, the boy felt strange tingles inside his body when he got covered by a small tornado. The boy saw sparks glistening and energy- zaps shot towards his body. He started to have a headache, like nothing he had ever felt before. It felt as if his brain was being squashed into a different shape but with some laser-like zaps.

Two minutes later ...

All the strange tingles, headaches, and zapping were gone. He seemed somehow 'different'.

Now he was like the magical people, but some aspects of his weird appearance were still there, Including the hypnotising face.

The boy then flew unstably around like a tourist that was lost and trying to get his sense of direction.

Soon enough, he finally found his way to a gigantic house marked:

S*CH: OO' L AC-AD)EMY

But the boy already knew that the writing stood for: *school academy*.

Out of nowhere, a slim, older woman with a long dress falling in folds appeared and stood in front of Rigel. She asked in a rush:

'What do you want? You should come in here, into the school and stabilise your

magic. You were flying so crazily that I thought you were a giant bug.'

The boy replied nervously:

'I want to go inside-'

'the school.' The woman finished the sentence and then she vanished into thin air.

***

The boy stood there, or rather hovered there, in a puzzled way. Then suddenly a voice startled Rigel:

'Hello *Rigel,* let me show you around the school.'

The boy was enchanted to hear that somebody had guessed his name. So he turned around and saw a kind-hearted-looking woman, with cracked, oval spectacles and an old wizard hat. The body of this teacher was oval, and she had thin legs, and each of her hands and feet had seven toes/fingers.

Rigel asked in a half-jittery and clueless way:

'How did you guess my name?'

'Oh, you will learn that trick' replied the woman. 'Anyway, do you want to check out the school?' she continued.

'Ummm, o-ok,' Rigel said in confusion.

The stranger stood in front of the boy and then walked into the school in fashion. The boy decided to follow her.

Once the boy was inside the school, he was mesmerised to see how beautiful it was.

The classrooms were decorated with diamonds or flowers either on their doors or around the edges of their windows. The classrooms had wizard hat-shaped and wave-shaped windows.

Some windows had writing's around the edges saying 'fairy'. Some of the windows were decorated with ribbons. Others were covered with beautiful patterns. Some walls had a few whiteboards for outdoor learning, but the others were covered with wands and calming lines.

Most of the walls were lighted with candles. Either pupil would hover and talk or fly stylishly to show off.

Some pupils around Rigel had hats to show that they were one of the *class 6* pupils. While the teachers wore different hats.

All of the classrooms were located on either the southwest or northeast wing of the school.

After being hypnotised by his tour of the school, the boy followed the teacher to the north. The teacher pointed to a faraway, gigantic door. It was difficult to tell how far away it was, but it was located northwest of the school.

'That is the hallway' the teacher explained.

The boy nodded.

The teacher then moved her index finger 40 degrees to the left and started pointing an old fashioned door not far away. The door was located southeast of the school.

'That is the teacher's lounge. Don't ever go inside there.' The teacher whispered.

The teacher, after that, flew to a door with toilet paper rolls all around it. It was located to the west.

'This is the toilet for boys and girls' she said.

The boy nodded again.

The teacher then turned her index finger 120 degrees anti-clockwise pointing to the only window. There was a playground through the window. The playground was located east of the school.

'That is the playground?' the boy said before the teacher could.

'Yes,' the teacher nodded. 'The pupils must play in the playground since things are so dangerous here.'

'Does the school have protection?' the boy asked nervously.

'Yes,' the teacher responded. 'It is some kind of mysterious power that does not let monsters or other dangerous creatures out of the school,' the teacher resumed.

'*Out* of the school? But... Anyway, how can it do that?' the boy asked.

'There is a scientific explanation,' the teacher said.

'What is the scientific explanation?' the boy asked.

'The protection is a mixture of dangerous creatures' blood and liquid that can recognise any dangerous monsters, making a powerful force to blast the monsters away' the teacher said without looking at the boy.

'How big is this school?' the boy questioned the teacher curiously, once more.

'The school covers about 260 square miles' the teacher responded.

'Wow ...' Rigel murmured, shocked.

After they had been walking for about three minutes, the teacher started pointing to a room covered with shining diamonds. It was at the northeast of the school. On the classroom door, there was a sign saying *class 1*.

'You will learn the basic tricks here,' said the teacher.

'What tricks?' the boy asked.

'Good question! They teach you superstrength, speed, agility, quick reflexes, toughness, supersenses, immortality, flight, healing, and other primary powers.'

'What do they use them for?' the boy wondered.

'Do you see that boy? the teacher said, pointing to a boy hiding behind a bush.

'Uhh, yes?' the boy said

'That boy is using supersenses to detect a fake roaring monster, and to find the best place to attack the monster' the teacher said.

'So this school is about *destroying* monsters?' the boy immediately asked.

'Correct' the teacher replied.

'What other examples are there?' the boy asked.

'Well, they learn teleportation at this school. Look there!' The index finger of the teacher pointed to a girl 25 meters away. 'That girl is using teleportation to escape that cut-out attacking monster. She is teleporting to that spare room' the teacher continued.

'Hmm ... Can you give me an example of ...' The boy paused for a second. 'Durability?'

'Let's see ... you see that twin? And that big silvery tank near her?' her index finger moved 30 degrees east of the previous girl.

Rigel nodded his head.

'They used the durability power against that tank,' replied the teacher.

'Can you explain a little more?'

'The tank continuously threatens to squash the pupils. That twin has escaped from it. To stop the tank, the twin uses the durability power.' the teacher replied.

'How long does it take pupils to learn to do basic tricks professionally?' the boy asked again.

'The average time should be between four and five months,' the teacher replied.

'In some other classes, pupils learn to do telepathy, teleportation, shapeshifting, X-ray vision, and other amazing stuff' the teacher added.

They then started to walk further towards an open area where they saw some other school staff members and pupils working on their magic. One of the pupils had just made a new type of magic!

The pupil called it *'the blaster ™.'* He mixed blasting fire with some 'illusion' hypnotiser liquid. If fire and hypnotiser liquid mix, they turn into such a powerful force that it could destroy 10,000 metric tons of monsters in 12,000 groups in just a second. Not only that, the power of the force could overwhelm all humans living on earth!

'Ummm, Miss!' the boy called anxiously. 'Something strange happened when I was playing near my house. Does it mean anything?'

'What?' the teacher asked.

The boy then started to tell the teacher about where he and his family were, how they were playing, the rising forest, the monster attacking, the disappearing of mom, dad, and sister, how he went into the forest and found his parents and sister, as well as discovered the path to this planet.

'Hmm, not much. But I guess that your parents and .... Wait ...' the teacher suddenly cut her sentence short. 'Is your sister called *Fooler*?' she continued.

'Yes?' the boy said, confused.

'No, she is not your sister.'

'What?' the boy responded incredulously.

'That is the wicked, unbeatable monster that ever lived' the teacher said to the boy's shock.

'Did I have a real sister?' asked the boy.

'She is trapped beneath layers of rock in an unknown underground cell.'

'What? When did this happen?'

'It was when you were about two years old' the teacher replied.

'How do you know that?'

'Because I watched over you,'

'Why?' the boy questioned seriously.

'Your great-great-grandfather was once the best guardian that ever protected us from those monsters, so we guessed that one day you would be one.'

'And how about my parents? I saw them sleeping in the enchanted forest with my sister' the boy responded.

'Your mother and father are only enchanted by the wicked monster and will be freed by a powerful fairy, and so will you' the teacher explained.

'The fairy? Me? Can I be a powerful fairy?' Rigel stopped for a second.

'Where did the fairy come from, and why did she come to save my parents?'

'I will explain it some other day. It is time for you to sleep.'

The teacher then led the boy to his new bed.

It was night, and all the pupils were going to bed, including Rigel.

When the boy saw the bed, he was shocked and stared in amazement. He saw a glowing green light and same realistic-looking human images lying on his bed. This immediately reminded of his parents. The bed was so comfortable that it felt like he was sitting on his *dream bed*'. There was nobody else in the room.

The boy went into the room nervously, and the teacher waved goodbye to him.

Half an hour later ...

The boy could not sleep, so he was looking out of the window, staring grumpily.

Unexpectedly, red flashes suddenly filled the magical window. The boy looked closely at the red flashes and through all the light. He then saw a dark monster shape of some kind. But the monster noticed the boy first, and the monster said some magic words:

'sleep ... sleep ... Don't remember anything, go back... go back to your dreams ...'

***

CHAPTER 2

The boy felt exhausted because of the terrible nightmare or maybe the spell. However, whoever made the spell had not noticed that the boy was *half-*human, half-fairy, so Rigel did not lose his memory when he got enchanted.

The boy sat up in bed and started to stare out of the window. He suddenly stopped staring, thinking for a moment about his beloved parents.

At a time like this at home, his parents would have helped him get ready for school. They would have made a delicious small pizza and given him a glass of cold apple juice for breakfast, his favourite. They would then have waved goodbye proudly as he was about to go to school.

Rigel whimpered remembering those moments. At the same time, he knew that his parents were asleep in a forest he had recently discovered. The boy told himself he had to be powerful enough to save his parents, so now he knew he had to go downstairs to learn the powers. He immediately stood up on his bed unstably, almost falling off.

After that, Rigel went downstairs and met the teacher who had showed him around the school the day before.

'Good morning Rigel.' The teacher was looking hard at the boy's face. 'What happened to you?' the teacher suddenly asked.

'Aargh.' Rigel complained. 'Last night a monster cast a spell on me, giving me a headache' the boy continued.

'Then how did you remember the time where you got this sort of spell cast on you?' the teacher said curiously.

'I am not sure.' Rigel paused for a second. 'I somehow remember it.'

'**BREAKFAST, BREAKFAST!!**'

A loud booming voice cut off their conversation.

'Is it time for breakfast?' the boy asked when the announcement had stopped.

'Yes it is,' replied the teacher.

Rigel and the teacher instantly started walking southeast of the school.

Half a mile from their destination, the lunch hall, an upside-down door glittered and a sign appeared over it saying: **CLASS 2**. That class would be the next study for the boy, tomorrow.

Around the upside-down door excited, chattering people would usually wait for class. The classroom looked small from the outside but gigantic once you were inside. The walls of *class 2* would be shining green filled with pictures of fairies and monsters fighting, a symbol of war.

Around the boy and the teacher, pupils either were flying to show-off or hovering while chatting to each other. The school roof displayed the history of the planet and fairies. Along the way, all the walls were mixed, purple, red, and gold, meaning peace.

Class 5 then came into sight when the teacher and the boy were halfway through their journey.

'Anyway, I was thinking about your name ... So what is your ... name?' Rigel broke the silence.

'My name is Lyra' the teacher answered.

'Oh, ok' the boy said confused, looking at the teacher.

Class 5's door was covered with rare, glittering diamonds, representing the environment. Protecting the environment was very important. In the '19s the fairies suffered from smoke, litter, and toxic waste, so in the early '20s, they decided to start to make the planet better. And if anybody does one of those things to hurt the environment, the fairy police would immediately send them to jail where they would stay until they die.

***

After *class 5*, they entered the dining hall.

The teacher and the boy sat on cushioned, glittering gold chairs that could produce all sorts of entertainment if the patient was bored. But just as they sat, a puff of steam hurtled from a decorated door with a sign over it saying:

: KIT/CH':: EN

Various fairies suddenly burst out of the door, holding silver plates. They looked very busy with serving.

'What was the smoke about?' the boy said curiously.

'That is a sign meaning 'take the plates'' the teacher replied immediately, licking her lips.

The fairies started to set out the plates on gigantic, hovering tables. Each table could seat about 300 trolls.

CLAP CLAP CLAP

'We will begin the banquet' said a man with straightened hair, a few wrinkles, one hypnotic eye, and a triangular face. He was sitting on an old-fashioned seat.

'That is the headmaster' Lyra whispered to Rigel.

The boy nodded.

Everyone licked their lips and then took the covers off of the silver plates.

The boy was shocked to see so many delicious kinds of food. There was a giant, hot turkey, small, delicious-smelling chickens, 200 on each plate. In the middle of the table, a tall silver cylinder stood with A glowing juice sloshing over the brim. A sign on it said:

SUPWERPOWE)((_(R JUI*()_+ CE

O(∩_∩)O

'Does this stuff give us ... (*munch ...*) more superpowers ... (*munch munch munch*)?' the boy asked, pointing to the juice while gobbling some tasty spicy green chips.

'Not really, the company who makes this kind of milk puts that sign on to attract people. The company is like a ...' Lyra paused for a second. 'It just has a **LOT** of money. But sometimes they get the 'boos!' though.' The teacher paused, searching for a mouth-watering morsel.

'Do they think that only *money* is important?' the boy asked with interest.

'Yes, they do' the teacher moaned to the sky.

'Have they got a lot of money?' the boy asked.

'Not even a single bit' the teacher answered.

'Can you give me that *delicious*-looking skillet cod with lemon and capers, *please?*' The boy suddenly stopped the conversation, pointing 35 degrees left of the giant chicken.

Suddenly, the skillet cod rose into the air and flew in front of Rigel, sticking onto his fork.

'Wow!' the boy said in amazement when the skillet cod finally stuck to the fork.

'No need to tell me to do it!' The teacher winked and grinned.

'Is that called *levitation*?' the boy asked.

'We call it *listening to levitation*' the teacher said whilst munching parmesan risotto with roasted prawns, another meal on the menu.

The teacher and the boy went off chomping some tasty food.

One hour later …

Rigel and the teacher cleaned their mouths with white tissues and walked off, greeting some pupils who were still eating mouth-watering food.

'You will first learn the basic tricks in this class today before you start learning in *class 2*' the teacher said when they arrived outside of a classroom. This was *class 1*.

The classroom had a crooked door, the (outside) wall was coloured yellow, meaning peace, while inside the classroom glowed with a candle-like light. The classroom was oval-shaped.

Rigel realised the teacher was not talking anymore. There was a long pause.

'Umm, sorry I was not listening to you carefully' the boy said quietly, staring at the wall.

'Why?' the teacher pretended not to know why the boy had not listened.

'Were you about to ask me why you suddenly felt tingles and zaps, and whether that is rare or not?' the teacher gave up, stopping herself from pretending more.

'Ho- how di-did y-yo-you know???' the boy responded, shocked.

'You will learn that trick here in this school' the teacher said.

'But is it rare?' the boy stared at the teacher curiously.

'It is rare, and it only happens each …' the teacher paused. 'Century' she continued.

'Who gets those strange tingles?' the boy asked.

'That only happens to our … savers!?' the teacher was shocked.

'When do the tingles happen?' the boy enquired.

'When the savers are young like you!'

'That means I am a …' the boy paused

'A saver, sooner or later!?' the teacher finished Rigels sentence

'What do they save?' the boy said as if he knew the answer.

'The *entire* planet, destroying all the monsters at that time. Anyway, I knew that just pretending.' The teacher whispered.

Out of nowhere, another teacher walked in and joined the conversation:

'Hello, Lyra and … new student?' the intruder said.

'Hello, Hydra.' Lyra greeted her.

The boy stared at Hydra, and he realised that Hydra and Lyra were identical twins. The only thing that made them different was their eyes. Lyra had blue eyes whilst Hydra had hazel eyes.

'What were you talking about, for fairy's sake?' Hydra asked.

'We were talking about the new saviour' Lyra answered.

'Who is it?' the other teacher asked excitedly.

'Am I supposed to be in this conversation?' The boy suddenly spoke.

'Sorry, we did not see you there!' Lyra responded.

'Are you ser … Oh fine.' The boy said, sounding grumpy with Lyra.

'Anyway, who Is our next saver?' Hydra asked interestedly.

'You might not believe who it is …' Lyra stopped for a second. 'It is this boy' she continued.

The boy pushed his belly out and grinned.

'You-you-you mean this-this b-b-boy?' Hydra could not believe her eyes.

'Yes, this boy, standing in front of you' Lyra said.

'....' Hydra could not answer, only stood there with her mouth open wide.

The boy and Lyra waved goodbye as Hydra walked away without comment.; Hydra still had her mouth open wide, about to spread the news.

'Anyway, here i-,' Lyra got cut off by the boy.

'Yes, yes, you told me that this is the place where I will study!' The boy rolled his eyes.

'... Oh yes,' the teacher finally remembered.

'**STUDY, STUDY, TIME TO STUDY!!!**'
a loudspeaker boomed somewhere.

'Time to go study, Rigel!' Lyra exclaimed. 'Have a good time.'

'Bye see you soon' the boy replied.

The boy then went into *class 1*. However, nobody was there, only a teacher reading a biography with his feet up on the table.

The walls of the classroom were coated in new paint, coloured royal blue, meaning will, the fairies thought.

The boy said '*hi*' shyly to the male teacher. The teacher replied, 'good morning', putting his book down.

The teacher had a muscular body, one gigantic foot (1 and a half metres in diameter), a trapezium eye with a bent iris, a pointed nose, a sharp ear, and a kite-shaped head.

'Today we will learn basic tricks for …' the teacher suddenly got cut off.

'-Super strength, speed, agility, and reflexes' the boy finished the teacher's sentence. He then glared at the teacher and continued at full speed. 'Durability, supersenses, immortality, flight, and healing.'

'No. That is too much' the teacher hissed.

'Then what?'

'You will only learn super strength, flying, healing, and immortality today.' The teacher looked at the boy then said. ''Anyway, let's start class.'' The anger drained out of the teacher's face.

'What will we learn first?' the boy asked excitedly.

'Let's test your super strength!' the teacher glared at the boy.

'OK.' The boy flew unstably but very fast towards the teacher.

'First, pick up this table and throw it into the air! Just smash the roof.' The teacher pointed to a table.

The table had bent legs, half of its drawers were gone, and it had a rectangular shape but with no edges. The tabletop looked burned, and it seemed to be made of willow.

The boy picked the table up with both hands, gripping it as hard as he could and just managed to do it, but when he tried to pick up the table with just his pinky finger, the table suddenly flew up into the air and smashed into the roof.

'Whoops!' the boy said embarrassedly.

Some beautiful birds flew through the window into the room and chirped a rhyme:

'Oh no, what happened? It looked good at first and ... then the tiles complained ...'

'Anyway, that was fine.' The teacher watched the birds fly away.

'Time for you to heal the roof' the teacher continued.

'What?' the boy looked shocked.

'Can healing even heal non-living things?' the boy asked.

'Yes, it can' the teacher grinned.

'But you have to improve your flying first before you learn to heal.' The teacher raised an eyebrow. 'You fly crazily' he resumed.

'All right' the boy sighed.

'I already know that you can take-off and land, but your flying is nuts' the teacher crossed his arms.

Rigel took off, flew out of the window to the playground, and asked the teacher how to control his flight.

'You have to adjust your arms so that they are straight to balance,' the teacher explained.

And the boy did what he was supposed to do.

It worked!

The boy smiled happily. He then flew over the playground straight and although he flew as fast as he could, he could not rise or turn.

'How do you turn?' the boy looked back through the window.

'You have to kick your legs in the opposite direction of the direction you want to go.' The teacher watched as the boy turned around in different directions.

'How do you fly higher?' the boy posed another question, curious.

'Put your hands neatly at your sides and you will start to rise slowly' the teacher shouted as the boy flew further up.

The boy did it.

Soon enough, he was up with the birds. The birds looked as if they were playing some kind of game, while the boy thought they were just flying and having fun. They were chirping something, but the boy could not understand what.

'**HOW DO YOU GET DOWN!!?**' the boy shouted loudly enough for the teacher to hear far below. He needed to go down immediately.

***

CHAPTER 3

'**MAKE A STAR SHAPE WITH YOUR WHOLE BODY. THAT SHOULD WORK!!!**' the teacher shouted back.

One minute later …

The boy arrived at the edge of the playground and was one metre above the grass. The boy flew back to class swiftly without mistakes.

CLAP CLAP CLAP

'Well done, *now* you have learnt how to fly properly!' the teacher smiled.

A slight pink grew across Rigel's cheeks. He was proud.

'Now that you know how to fly, time to learn to heal!' the teacher said.

'Cool' the boy nodded.

'Fly up there! And do as I say' the teacher looked at the boy suspiciously.

The boy jumped and got himself into the 'arms at your sides' position as he did.

He then started to fly upwards towards the broken roof.

'What do I do now?' the boy asked the teacher.

'Put your hands on the broken tile, say 'heal' in any language and imagine you are healing something, anything!' the teacher shouted back.

The boy put his hands on the tile and softly said 'Xianer.' At the same time, he closed his eyes and imagined healing a person with a cut on his forehead.

Out of nowhere, the cracks started to get narrower and narrower, and the big hole slowly shrank. A deep humming sound grew louder and louder each second. some blasts of blue, red, and green light shot out, whistling, healing the cracks. The roof was starting to turn into the 'fairy's history display'. Tiles appeared out of nowhere and glued firmly across the hole, restoring it to its original shape.

Four minutes later …

The roof had been fixed with the help of healing. The boy stared at the tiles, and the tiles looked precisely like the *old* tiles. There was nothing 'new' in them. The boy then glared at the teacher who was looking proud.

'I d-di-did it' the boy unbelievingly said hovering beside the fixed roof.

'Amazing! Nobody has passed the healing test their first time … Only our saviours.' The teacher glanced at the boy, realising something ...

'The boy had passed the healing test his first time, and that only happens to our saviours ... It can only have one meaning...' The teacher thought surprised.

'Ummm... hello!? Don't think about the next saver' the boy warned.

That sentence jolted the teacher into action and all of a sudden and he replied:

'Sorry, sorry, but well done, that was amazing work!' The teacher had a trickle sweat going down from his left eyebrow.

The boy grinned, his eyes gleaming, and put his hands down by his sides.

'But what next?' the boy asked excitedly.

'Now it's time to learn im-' something crashed into the roof, cutting the teacher off mid-sentence.

CRASH BANG BOOM!!!!!!!!!!!!!

On the floor, a cannon had appeared, a magical cannon as the boy thought. It had a rusty cuboid body, a hemisphere bottom, and a metalic rope hung from the bottom, wiggling. The cannon could hover because the hemisphere bottom made it fly.

'-Immortality!' the teacher finished his sentence looked at the cannon in surprise.

'Wow ... *That* is gonna be interesting.' The boy looked down, observing the cannon.

'Yes, it is.' The teacher replied.

Something then blinged inside Rigel's head. *'We could use the cannon to hit me to train me in the way to gain immortality'* the boy thought scanning the length of the cannon just to make sure there were no traps or anything.

'Can we use the cannon to shoot me for immortality training?' the boy asked.

'Great idea!' the teacher exclaimed.

'Can we-' the boy got cut off by the teacher.

'Wait, let me get the *automatic matches*.' The teacher dug through a rusty box lying in a pile of dust in the corner of the room.

Soon, the teacher found a matchstick and walked over to the cannon. The boy flew downwards with his body in the star shape, meeting the teacher.

'Are you ready?' the teacher asked.

'Read-' the boy paused.

'Wait, how do we get ready for immortality?' the boy asked.

'Just let out all your powers when the blow hits?' the teacher explained, but it sounded like a question as much as an explanation.

'Ok ...' The boy was surveying his entire body to make sure that he was well prepared. 'I am ready' he said bravely.

The teacher looked into the cannon and found a cannonball deep inside it. The teacher took out one of the matchsticks, put it near the rope, and the match immediately burst into flame.

Less than two seconds later…

The cannonball flew straight towards Rigel, striking him directly in the chest.

Rigel let as many powers out of his body as he could. Whew...

BOOM!!

The ball hit the boy with such force that he almost got knocked out, but luckily the 'take out powers' move saved his life.

The boy struggled to stand up.

'I-I d-did it' the boy half grunted, half amazed, half proud.

'Am-am- amazing' the teacher could not believe it. He was examining the boy just to make sure there were no broken bones.

'Did I do it? Did I *really* do it??' the boy said, staring at himself, doing the same thing as the teacher.

'Yes … You just passed the first test.' The teacher walked to his desk.

'For today?' the boy corrected the teacher.

'Yes.' The teacher went back to reading the biography.

'I just walk out?'

'Just go...'. The teacher seemed grumpy.

The boy walked out of the class and stared back, confused.

But just then out of nowhere, a figure flashed near a door. The figure walked towards the boy. Rigel soon realised it was a pupil, the pupil he met yesterday, and he was making his own type of magic.

'Hello,' he said mysteriously. 'Take this!' he resumed abruptly.

'What is this?' the boy replied, puzzled.

Rigel then examined what he had been given and saw that it was a fortune cookie. He opened it up and it started to spark red. Then all he saw was white.

***

The next morning, the boy woke up suddenly in his bed. Something terrible had happened last night. Somebody gave him a fortune cookie and then everything went blurry, and he could not remember anything else.

What he was really sure of was his dream. Rigel had dreamt about a monster who had been wanting to kill him. Rigel The monster had been hiding in the school for years, waiting for Rigel. The monster already knew that Rigel was the next saviour. In the dream a voice said that the creature was the one who sent the monsters into the real world, to make Rigel enter the magical world. The monster in the school would kill Rigel and then destroy the magic world. The monster had tried several times before to kill other saviours, but he had failed. But the deadly creature believed he had a chance to destroy the boy...

Rigel was thinking in his head:

'Did something worse happen than the 'fortune cookie'? The dream felt so real ...'.

Rigel decided to go to Lyra. The only thing making the boy feel safe was being with Lyra. The boy wanted to ask her what had happened.

He walked along his bed, feeling strange. He suddenly realised that he smelt fresh blood. Rigel was feeling scared, and he immediately heard people shrieking somewhere. He was trembling

BOOM!!!

He was outside his room now. The boy saw lightning strike the ground.

Rigel tripped on the creaky stairs shuddering with trepidation.

When he got downstairs, he found Lyra. She was smiling, but there was something wrong, her teeth were pointed, unlike the rectangular ones. The boy was more frightened than ever.

'Good mor-*growl* morning' she grunted.

'Good... mor-mor-morning' the boy replied.

'Let's go eat breakfast' she grinned.

'Our real teacher does not say that immediately, she normally has a little

conversation with us and the announcements have not started yet' the boy thought.

'OK.' The boy glared at the teacher suspiciously.

The teacher walked through the red, gold, and purple maze of walls.

One minute later …

The boy saw a male pupil passing him. The pupil was short with almost white hair. He nodded at Rigel with a wink, and Rigel realised that he wanted to be friends with him. So Rigel waved at the pupil.

The pupil was not only short but had a flat body, thin arms, and a triangular face under his almost-black hair. All of a sudden, the teacher glared at the boy furiously.

Rigel was not sure why.

After two minutes passed, Rigel saw another pupil wink at him. This time, it was a female pupil. She had a round, kind face, short, dark hair, a long, thin, elegant body, an oval head, and pentagon-shaped feet covered by transparent shoes. Again, the teacher glared at the boy madly. The boy suddenly realised that he had passed the hallway he would usually have gone down. He was going much faster than usual.

'Wait, we passed the hallway.' The boy interrupted the silence with a frowned face.

The teacher gave the boy a grim stare and walked the opposite way away from Rigel.

'*This is strange*' the boy thought.

They were walking past a few doors, but those doors were ... Squealing. The boy was so confused hearing that.

'GROWL GROWL!'

Suddenly, a weird, growling voice echoed along the hallway. It looked as if it was coming from the teacher, but she tried to hide it from the boy.

Rigel glanced suspiciously at the teacher. She responded with a whistle and rolled her eyes.

One minute later ...

The boy saw another pupil wink at him. The boy gave a wink too. Rigel soon realised that each pupil he met had the same t-shirt on. The t-shirts all had yellow stars and red hearts on a black background.

'*Are they a team?*' the boy asked himself. '*Maybe,*' Rigel answered in his head.

Just then, the announcer shouted, and Rigel and the teacher both arrived at the hallway leading to the breakfast room.

BREAKFAST BREAKFAST!!!

A crowd of people with licking tongues went rushing down the hallway. The teacher and the boy got squeezed flat in the chaos.

In less than a second, the teacher and the boy were already in their seats in the breakfast-room. Smoke started to pour out of the kitchen door. As expected, fairies gushed out of the door, with shining, silver plates.

On the tables, the fairies put the plates and uncovered them. Everyone was starting to gobble up the food. But there was something strange going on. The only thing the teacher was eating was *meat*, nothing else.

The boy took a quick peek at the teacher before Lyra could look up from her food and stare back. Something made the boy tremble. He saw a half-hidden red horn pointing out of her hat. The boy suddenly realised something. The teacher was not talking to the boy when they had been in the hallway. Instead, she had been talking to the air without the boy knowing.

'Does that mean she was talking to … *somebody else?'* the boy murmured. *'I found strange devilish stuff firmly stuck on L-L-Ly-Lyra?!'* He continued thinking.

'Oh no … That means … this 'Lyra' is not the real Lyra. Whoever s/he is, the stranger might have locked the real Lyra. And the

*thin air she is talking to is ... maybe an invisible **monster**? So that Lyra **is** a monster.'* Suspicious thoughts kept bothering him.

Rigel quickly gobbled up a mozzarella pizza and walked away. The teacher did not say 'See you soon!' She was still talking to the thin air. *'This is even stranger.'* the boy thought, glaring at the teacher.

When he arrived at the doors of the hall, he saw another female pupil wink at him. This time the pupil's T-shirt had only one heart and one star.

Something blinged inside Rigel's head. *'Do they want to be my friends?'* The boy looked back at the female pupil.

Rigel saw the pupil walking towards a door and going inside. The pupil did not firmly close the door, though. The boy then walked away.

'Pppsst.' Suddenly, a voice echoed along the hallway.

The boy cocked his head. He saw the male pupil he had met before. He was next to the door where the female pupil had gone in.

'What?' The boy rolled his eyes.

'Come here!' the pupil replied.

'Why?' the boy asked.

'It is important.' The pupil rushed his sentence.

The boy swiftly turned around and walked cautiously towards the door.

Before Rigel could even reach the door, the pupil grabbed him and pushed him through a white door next to the door

Rigel had been heading for into a brilliantly white room. The door was marked **PURITY**. Rigel was about to ask the pupil why the walls were so white, but the boy had already read his mind, so he just said 'Nevermind'.

When the boy stepped into the room, all the pupil he had met earlier appeared out of nowhere.

'**HI!**' they all said at once.

'H-h-hi??' the boy answered, confused.

'We all know that you discovered your teacher was acting weird, like a monster' a female pupil continued.

'Yes.' The boy was shocked to see somebody knew his secret. 'But what is all this about?' he demanded.

'We formed this team when we found out that you were in … danger' a male pupil said.

'But can I be your …'. The boy paused. 'Your friend?' the boy rubbed his head.

'Yes, we were also about to say that' somebody said.

'What are we going to do?' the boy asked.

'We will fight the monsters' another said fiercely.

'But I only know a few magic'-'somebody cut off his sentence.

'You are the next saviour. This team was formed to protect you' somebody else interrupted.

'Ho-h-h-h-how, did you know?'

The boy was stunned.

'We spied on you'-'a pupil said but got cut off by Rigel.

'Like the real Lyra?' Rigel asked.

'She let us join her spying' a pupil sighed.

'But who … no …what are your names?' the boy asked.

'I am Cygnus' a thin boy that Rigel met first replied. Cygnus had a parallelogram-shaped head, a skinny body, almost flat, spiked arms and legs, drooping ears, rhombus eyes with thin yellow pupils, an almost invisible peach mouth, and tidy brown hair. He had no nose.

'I am Auriga' a female pupil said. Rigel had met her before as well. Auriga had a transparent body, fragile arms and legs, a triangle-shaped head, pointed ears, cloud-like eyes with hypnotising pupils, gold lipstick on her lips, a curled nose, and four short plaits.

'I am Sagittarius' a male pupil waved. Saggitarius had a muscular body, substantial arms and legs, a rectangular-shaped head, leaf-like ears, circular eyes with purple pupils, a triangular nose, and long red, purple, and brown hair.

'And I am Phoenix, the leader' another female proudly said. Phoenix had a half thin, half muscular body, weak arms, thick legs, an impossibly-complexly-shaped angular head, 'L'-shaped ears, dark red lipstick on her lips, and blob-like eyes with serious, dark pupils. Her hair was of all types at once (ponytails, plaits, bobs, and other styles).

'So, you are Cygnus, you are Auriga, you are Sagittarius, and you are

Phoenix.' The boy was pointing at all of the pupils.

'YES.' They all nodded.

'What are we going to do *now*?' the boy asked.

'We are going to…' Cygnus paused.

'What are we going to do?' Cygnus whispered to Phoenix.

'We are going to check out the 'monster'' Phoenix answered.

'And what am *I* going to do?' the boy asked.

'You are going to be our detector' Phoenix answered.

'But I only know how to heal, fly, be immortal, and have super strength.' The boy was confused.

'No, did you know that in healing you can detect monster blood?' Phoenix asked the boy.

'No, I didn't know that' Rigel responded. 'So that is why I could smell some strange stuff when I was healing the roof?'

'Yes …'. Phoenix rubbed her hands. 'Anyway, let's start!'

Something instantly smelled strange to the boy. '*I smell monster blood*' the boy thought.

***

CHAPTER 4

'This way' Rigel said automatically, pointing northwest of the school.

The team, including the boy, ran to the door pointing north. After that, they ran northwest of the school.

'Wait, wait, wait.' The boy stopped in front of the door.

'WHAT?' The team halted.

'You said I could smell monster blood with healing, right?' The boy gazed at the team.

'Yes…'. Phoenix rolled her eyes.

'If I can smell monster blood, then it might be another monster instead of

'Lyra', maybe another monster luring us into danger' the boy explained.

'Great point. We did not think of that.' Sagittarius rubbed his head.

'Then what are we going to do?' the boy enquired.

Phoenix thought for a while and then shrugged. The boy cocked an eyebrow.

'Listen here 'boy' I am the leader; nobody makes suggestions only me.' Somebody said in Rigel's head.

The boy looked at Phoenix. She was now looking quite furious. Rigel could almost see fumes coming from her mouth when Rigel realised that Phoenix *was* the one who said something in his head. So, the boy glared 'I give up' at Phoenix, a look that said he had surrendered himself to agreeing that Phoenix was the leader.

However, the team just continued walking as if they knew what had happened. Phoenix instantly smirked and moved to the front of the team, showing the way. Rigel chose to follow them as they headed northwest.

Ten minutes later …

'Sniff sniff.' The boy smelled the air, then the path.

'Wait…' the boy warned the team. 'Now the monster is going southeast, heading right towards us' he resumed.

Phoenix nodded, agreeing with Rigel, and walked northwest immediately.

The team followed Phoenix.

'Wow, Phoenix is really a 'leader'.' The boy thought, probably teasing Phoenix

'What did you just think about me?!' Phoenix asked the boy, urgently.

'No-no-nothing' the boy replied.

Phoenix gave Rigel a hard glare, so the boy decided to quit the conversation.

They walked through a maze of red, gold, and purple walls.

'Pppstt …' the boy whispered to the team as they walked along. They had been walking for about ten minutes.

'Yes?' the team answered.

'Lyra is there' the boy said, pointing to a half-monster and half-human figure.

The team nodded and walked straight towards the monster. They were now behind the drooling creature. Sagittarius took out a kind of purple pistol which he had recently made and pointed it directly at the monster.

The monster had a brown-green muscular body, crooked legs, a pair of super-strong brown-green arms, a third ordinary human arm, a dark green toothpick-shaped head (but with no sharp points), attached on a half-oval head, two hands (on a pair of two arms) and foot with three purple-brown fingers and toes and very long nails, one hand and foot with seven fingers/toes, one unimaginably bright eye and another ordinary eye. The monster also had a ripped ear and a pointed ear.

Soon enough, Sagittarius shot at the monster. But the monster turned around and caught the pistol in its megalodon-like teeth and threw it so hard it flew twice the speed of the bullet, more than 120 miles per hour, straight into the roof.

BOOM!

The pistol easily broke most of the tiles in the school, making a 5 wide-mile hole. But it made a silent *boom* so no one noticed.

The team was shocked to see such a big hole.

Some of the birds outside the broken roof got injured, making blue sparks drain from their bodies. The lit-up 'history display' on the roof started to grow dark. The edges of the ruined roof were now dark brown, and a dingy smoke was beginning to cover the edge nearest to the team and the monster. Most of the tiles were cracked to pieces, falling to the ground like rain.

The team walked backwards, not daring to turn around but retreating from the impact.

After that, the monster turned around, looking hard at the team with a dangerous glare.

'H*ow-growl,* ***dare y****-growl* ***you!***'

The monster alarmed the team.

But before the evil creature could eat the team, Rigel sprang into action. He was mad because the shot had missed. So he flew at ultra-speed heading directly towards the monster without hesitation. Rigel took a tile from the floor and slapped the monster with such force that it sent the monster towards the hole. The monster tried to stop but got propelled by the 1,000 x G g-force that Rigel's move had made.

After the 'fight' the team clapped.

CLAP CLAP

'Well done, that will buy us a few minutes to make a plan before the monster comes to' Phoenix thanked Rigel.

'But did you see that the creature tried to shield herself from the sunlight? That means ...'. Rigel paused.

'She hates the light.' Cygnus finished Rigel's sentence.

'We have a plan' Phoenix said.

BESIDE THE SCHOOL WHERE THE MONSTER IS

The creature woke up from being stunned by the impact, regaining consciousness. It sat there on a pile of red tiles struggling to tell the history of the fairies. when the roof started talking about how dangerous monsters were,

The monster got so annoyed that it smashed the tiles into even more pieces.

'HOW DARE THEY; NOW I *WILL* TAKE REVENGE!' the monster shouted to the thin air, darkening the sunlight.

The creature saw something familiar, but it soon disappeared. It got up and walked towards the school before flying up into the air.

THE TEAM: BEFORE THE MONSTER WOKE UP

'The plan is to collect as much sunlight as we can so we can blind the monster for an hour at least' Phoenix explained.

The boy took out a torch from his pocket. Rigel had got the torch from somebody called Perseus. Perseus was cool, as the boy thought. He had slick hair, looked a lot like Rigel, and made funny but scary jokes.

Rigel had coincidentally met him before he entered the fairies' world. For no reason, he came to Rigel's house, where they started to become friends. Somehow, the boy still had the torch when he fought the monsters near his house on that mesmerising day.

'This is a torch, and I think it has 400 Watts of power, as Perseus said.' The boy showed the team the torch.

'Per … seus?' Auriga looked stunned.

'Per … what?' Sagittarius was also astonished.

'Per … I can't believe it.' It looked like Cygnus was about to faint.

'PER … SEUS??!!' Phoenix said with opened mouth.

'Yes, Perseus, a bit like … my best friend … anyway, why are you all amazed?' Rigel asked the team.

'Perseus is the uncle of the 'monster Lyra'' Auriga eventually explained.

'The uncle of-yes-yes-yes … Wait, the uncle is the uncle of … the monster Lyra?' the boy jumped, looking flabbergasted.

'Yes,' Auriga replied.

'Hope that torch aint' be evil,' Cygnus all of a sudden was talking like a cowboy.

'We have to scan the torch just to make sure.' Auriga glared at the torch.

Auriga snatched the torch after putting on a pair of her handmade safety gloves. Suddenly glowing lava-hot colours started to spread like lava over Auriga's arm. Her body started to tingle and the tingling spread in different directions.

'GRO-ARH-GROWL.' Auriga started to walk like a zombie.

'What happened?' Rigel asked Phoenix, looking alarmed.

'That liquid is illegal on this planet. It can affect most people' Phoenix said, walking backwards away from Auriga.

'Fortunately, nobody else knows what the cure is to stop these diseases but we do. The cure is easy. Watch.' Phoenix started to spray something that looked like red water.

Auriga instantly stopped growling and smiled, a half-nervous, half-shy smile.

'What do you call that liquid?' the boy asked Phoenix after Auriga smiled.

'We call that *watire*.' Phoenix scanned Auriga's body.

'Is it a mixture of fire and water?' Rigel asked Phoenix.

'Yes,' Auriga interrupted.

'But the torch thing.... whatever is dangerous, so maybe we should not use it' Auriga said.

'*Torch*.' The boy corrected Auriga.

'I don't care. Anyway, what power should we use to fight the monster?' Auriga asked the team.

'Lightning power!' Cygnus instantly responded.

'Wait ...' the boy paused.

'Why didn't you use other powers, instead of only using a gun?' Rigel suddenly demanded.

'Because the monster can control other people's power if they are using it, like us, but not superstrength or invisibility. The monster can choose if she wants to control a power or not' Cygnus sighed.

'Then why did you not use superstrength and invisibility first?' The boy glared.

'We did not realise it until you did it' Phoenix interrupted, pointing to Rigel.

'Should I check the monster?' Auriga suddenly asked.

'Yes,' Phoenix agreed.

Auriga took off into the air, flying in the same direction as the monster got pulled by the huge g-force.

BESIDE THE SCHOOL

Auriga looked down at the deserted monster; he was waking up. Auriga saw some bruises on his head and arms. The monster had several wounds in his heart, and the bleeding made a huge streak down his chest.

From above, the monster was seen smashing something that looked like whining red paint.

Auriga instantly saw that the monster was looking at her, so she made herself invisible.

Auriga heard the monster say something. It only sounded like an insult.

After a few minutes ...

Auriga saw that the monster was flying back inside the school, so she went back to the team just to warn them.

WHEN AURIGA WARNED THE TEAM

'Guys…' Auriga had almost run out of breath.

'The monster is coming towards us' Auriga raised the alarm with the team.

'Quick, hide!' Phoenix commanded the team.

The team ran to a room with a sign saying *class 4*, although Rigel chose another room with a sign saying *Toilet*. He walked inside and shut the door. Both the team and Rigel looked around for protection, and the team found a table and Rigel found a hovering chair to hide under.

Soon, the monster landed below the broken tile, looking very mad. It glared around, growling in frustration. The monster used X-ray vision to look through walls. Finally, the monster found the team and Rigel.

'*I will destroy that boy first before killing that annoying team*' the monster thought.

It stomped over to the toilet, ripped open the door and found Rigel.

'F-*GROWL* food!' The monster licked his lips.

Rigel tried to run, but he immediately found he was stuck inside a ring of fire.

'*I have... no escape*' the boy thought.

Suddenly, the boy had an idea. He squashed his face into different shape using healing technique and made him look a lot like a pupil, unlike the way Rigel usually looked.

'*The healing can do so many stuff*' Rigel murmured surprisingly.

The monster stomped inside the toilet.

'He-' the monster got cut off.

'*I* am a pupil, not your victim.' Rigel imitated a pupil.

The monster rubbed his head in confusion.

'Where is he?' the monster finally said.

'On top of the sun,' the boy responded.

'The ...' the monster paused.

'The... what?' the monster looked flabbergasted.

'On top of the sun' Rigel said again.

The monster walked to the window, stared, turned to leave, but suddenly spotted the boy as it was going away.

'You are the boy!' the monster roared when he realised the 'pupil' was *the boy*.

The monster suddenly felt somebody coming towards him, about to attack him. *'The person is going to use water! S/he is going to attack with water, which I hate!'* the creature thought.

Just then, out of nowhere, water struck the monster and the creature slipped. It looked up ...

WHEN THE MONSTER ARRIVED IN SCHOOL: *CLASS 4*

'Rigel went to the other room. The creature will kill the boy first, then us.' Auriga scanned all over the place

'He is the next saviour, so we need to save him...' Phoenix gasped. 'Before he gets murdered!' Phoenix continued.

'We need a plan, another plan!' Phoenix clasped her hands.

The team thought for a while.

Three minutes later ...

'I have a plan!' Cygnus finally said.

'What?' the team asked curiously.

'We use water to trip him, and I know he also hates water so it will be a torture. We get a mirror and we reflect light onto the monster directly. Then we use lightning to shoot at him before throwing him out of the window, far away. We can probably use our magic to fling him into the sun!' Cygnus explained.

'Great!' Phoenix agreed.

'When will we start?' Phoenix asked.

'Now' Auriga instantly responded. 'Time to go' she resumed.

The team slowly flew to the toilet and went inside with no sound. The monster was beside Rigel, who was trapped inside the 'fire ring'.

Sagittarius sprayed some water on the monster. The monster looked up and saw Sagittarius. Immediately, the monster shot out a tangle of fire. It was so hot it was transparent. Sagittarius got captured. The fire started to get hotter and hotter. Sagittarius struggled to escape from the blazing fire. Auriga ran to Sagittarius to help and sprayed as much cold water at the fire as she could to cool it down. But the fire instantly turned into rock. The rock was huge and heavy and it went flying down onto Auriga, a perfect hit.

Auriga got knocked out for a few minutes.

'The plan looks to be more difficult than it seemed' Phoenix sighed, watching the brutal battle.

Rigel saw the fight through the transparent fire. The creature was winning! Rigel decided to help: he flew upwards as fast as he could before the fire could grow bigger, blocking the path. The boy looked around and found a broken mirror on the floor. Rigel took it and directed the sunlight into the eyes of the monster It went crazy. The monster started to run, breaking some toilet seats.

The monster was pressing his hands over its eyes.

Auriga finally woke up. She blasted lightning at the monster. Unfortunately, instead of hitting the monster, the lightning hit a mirror beside the monster, and it reflected the lightning, and it went at ultra-speed, hitting the fire tangled up around Sagittarius instead of the monster.

What the team did not know was that the fire turns suddenly to acid if hit by lightning.

The fire turned into acid and the acid was starting to melt Sagittarius's waist. He was starting to lose consciousness.

The boy shot a small amount of water at the acid, and as Rigel thought might happen, the acid started to disappear. The boy quickly flew to Sagittarius after the acid had completely disappeared. Rigel healed Sagittarius's melting waist.

From somewhere, the team heard a peaceful humming starting. It sang a song which is traditional in the fairy world. Blue, red, and green sparks were dancing around Sagittarius's waist, making mesmerising patterns. His waist stopped melting, instead, growing thicker into its previous shape. Some of the humming and light patterns stopped when Sagittarius's waist shape was healed.

Rigel was waiting for Sagittarius to wake up.

After several minutes…

Sagittarius's awareness started to grow. He was waking up. Sagittarius finally woke up. He was now conscious. Sagittarius looked around the 'battlefield.' He saw water leaking out of the toilet and broken mirrors. He also saw the blinded monster.

'Hi. This is just the beginning of the fight.' The boy gazed at the blinded monster while he held Sagittarius so he would not fall.

'H-hi' Sagittarius replied, wriggling out of Rigel's hands before flying towards the blinded creature.

Sagittarius flew in front of the creature.

'Hi *ugly*... whatever' Sagittarius insulted the monster.

Before the monster could insult Sagittarius back, it got hit by lightning. The monster was utterly unconscious for now.

'We're safe *now*',' Phoenix said.

'WHY DID YOU NOT HELP US!?' Rigel, Sagittarius, and Auriga confronted Phoenix and Cygnus.

Phoenix replied with a shrug.

'Now it is your turn! Pick up the monster and throw him into the sun!' Rigel demanded.

'Fine.' But Phoenix and Cygnus hesitated.

***

'Done.' Phoenix and Cygnus came back.

'You have put the monster into the sun?' Auriga asked them.

'Yes…' they groaned loudly.

'Then time to find the real Lyra!' Rigel said.

'WHAT?' Phoenix and Cygnus said, not believing what they had just heard.

'Yes.' The boy rolled his eyes.

The team walked out of the broken door. Suddenly, somebody stepped in front of the team, with a half proud and half nervous face.

***

CHAPTER 5

There stood the headmaster. He looked down at the tired team.

'You have just missed class, all of you!' the headmaster said in a low voice.

'Sorry, we just'- 'Phoenix got cut off.

'But well done for beating a dangerous monster, although there is one problem.' The headmaster coughed.

'What?' Phoenix asked the headmaster.

'You put the terrible creature into the sun, right?' the headmaster said.

'Yes,' Phoenix replied nervously.

'Then the monster will take energy from the sun so that later it will have 12 times its normal power.' The headmaster spoke calmly, but with a bit of fright in his voice.

'What?' Phoenix was speechless.

'What are we supposed to do then?' Phoenix finally said.

'Are we still meant to find Lyra?' Auriga interrupted the conversation.

'Wait! We are talking here!' Phoenix hissed back.

'Great, finding the real Lyra is a good idea' he headmaster beamed.

Is the headmaster on my side, instead of that annoying bunch?' Phoenix thought.

'Wait, did you know about our fight?' Phoenix asked the headmaster.

'Yes.' The headmaster settled on his chair again.

'But why do'- 'Phoenix got cut off.

'Let's just go already.' Rigel rolled his eyes.

'Fine...' Phoenix sighed.

'Wait, let me show you a map.' The headmaster gave them an old map.

'That was weird. The headmaster does not talk that way and does not give easy tasks; this is an easy task: the map *helps* us' Phoenix whispered after waving goodbye to the headmaster.

'He might be another monster?' Rigel wondered aloud.

'Maybe' Sagittarius said.

The team walked the way the map showed. It led through the playground and into a deserted but noisy forest. They heard some loud banging sounds coming from the muddy ground. There were growling sounds echoing around the forest. They found danger signs saying:

BE CAREFUL: MONSTER TERRITORY and so on.

The team walked northeast, south, and then northwest where they found some unknown animals. Bushes were all types of shapes, and all of them were devil red.

One hour later …

They found the place. 'The place' looked like a plain, rusty trapdoor. The team cautiously opened it. In the dark, there stood a monster licking its fiery lips.

'I now think that the headmaster *is* a monster' Rigel agreed.

'He is a madman.' Phoenix insulted the headmaster.

'Let's shut the door' Sagittarius proposed.

'Yes.' Cygnus shut the door immediately.

'I don't think this is the right place.' Rigel checked the map.

'Wait, look here.' Rigel pointed to a caption in very tiny type saying: *not here, Lyra is not here*.

'Of course!' Phoenix jumped.

'This *is* the real map, just a bit of ...' Phoenix thought for a second. '... editing' she continued. 'And here is a sentence saying *not here Lyra is not here*. So that means Lyra *is* here.' Phoenix guessed.

'Correct.' Rigel walked southwest.

'Another hour-long journey.' Auriga rolled her eyes tiredly.

The team walked back through the devil bushes where they found more weird insects. Trees looked like they had frowning eyes and mouths; each branch had a shape similar to hands about to catch the team. Some sort of voice was talking beneath the trees, sounding like hisses. Each step made a *sploosh creek, like* feet walking on planks above splashing waves.

A few hours later …

'Oh, we are finally here.' Rigel scanned the map.

'Look, another trapdoor.' Phoenix pointed to the ground excitedly.

The team immediately opened the trapdoor where they found …

Nothing.

'Another trap.' Auriga rolled her eyes once more.

'Well, I guess...' the boy sighed '… this is not the real map' he resumed with frustration, about to rip the map.

'Wait! We have not checked the *monster pit* carefully. We should check it' Phoenix said with a singular glint of excitement.

'What? Another hour-long journey!?' Auriga hesitated.

The team ignored her.

'Time to go.' Sagittarius walked away.

The team walked back through the forest, finding insects as big as their heads, walking through *living* trees, and finally finding the devilish bushes. The team eventually found the trapdoor, and there was something strange there.

On top of the trapdoor, there was a map. It looked like somebody had had a battle in the forest around the trapdoor. The trees looked burned and almost destroyed.

The team looked around in amazement.

Rigel opened the trapdoor after picking up the map and putting it neatly on the floor. Inside the trapdoor stood a monster even more powerful than the one they had fought last time. It filled the whole tunnel. The monster was about to pounce. The team walked backwards nervously. The monster then crawled through the tunnel and almost captured the whole team with his sticky hands and poisonous claws. The team then saw there were more monsters! Each monster growled with hunger.

The tunnel was slippery, making the monster who pounced on the team slid, crashing into other creatures.

For a couple of seconds, the team was safe.

Just then, a voice echoed through the misty tunnel. The sound sounded something like ...

Help!

Help!

Help!

Rigel looked at the map and then walked slowly into the dense darkness of the entrance to a different tunnel. Rigel stopped immediately.

That map showed another route, a new hint. The boy then picked the map up and walked in the direction where an X mark had appeared. Rigel unfolded the map to show the team.

'This map has to be the real one and the other has to be a fake.' Phoenix scanned the map from top to bottom.

The team instantly walked southeast: the direction of the route shown on the map. Rigel followed with Phoenix.

The team also found something had happened to the whole forest. It was no longer devilish. It was brighter. The team walked through the sunny forest admiring its appearance. The bushes had turned green, insects were now ordinary, and the tree-sculptures were turning into smiles.

The team soon found a door appearing slowly in the trees. There was a sign saying something, but it just looked like some neat but illegible scribbles. The team were about to open it all together.

But suddenly, the door disappeared mysteriously, with no trace. Sagittarius looked back at the map. The X had moved to a different location. 'We have to catch up with that door!' Auriga sighed.

''I *can help you*' a robotic voice from somewhere in the trees suddenly said.

Auriga looked around, startled.

'I am here, the map! I am the map' the robotic voice said again.

 The team and Auriga looked at the map.

'*Hello,*' the map said with a glowing smile appearing across its bottom edge.

The *map* turned suddenly into a human shape with human size. The team walked slowly backwards away from the *map*.

'*I will help you catch that supersonic door. Call me… Harita.*' The map bowed.

'He-hello' Sagittarius replied, confused.

'*Go inside me!*' Harita morphed into a door.

The team opened and walked through the *map* door. They found themselves in a luxurious room. Inside was a polished, white sofa, a transparent glass table on which rested some brightly-coloured mouth-watering fruits. Beyond the table, an old-fashioned window somehow showed a bird's-eye view of the forest. From the sky, it looked heavenly. They saw some green peaks of small mountains with clean snow at their very top, blue lakes, and all-around nature was mesmerising colours.

'*Enjoy!.*' Harita smiled from inside.

'How fast can you … 'Phoenix paused. 'Fly?' he continued while scanning the room.

Out of nowhere, a screen appeared, hovering above the table. It showed how fast the map was going, the surroundings, the real weather, and a route. The team was amazed, although Rigel was confused about the weather.

'The weather is … MULT weather?' Rigel read.

'MULT weather is all the different kinds of weather combined into one. It is rare in this world.' Auriga munched an apple.

'This weather is weird.' Rigel frowned at the screen.

'Wait, let me open the window' Phoenix suggested.

Phoenix walked to the 'birds-eye view' window. She grabbed the brown sculptured handle and pulled it upwards. Phoenix's lips instantly flapped like crazy because they all were going at an immense speed. All Phoenix saw was blurry, a mix of different shades of different colours. Everyone's hair started to flap in the wind.

'I SH-BLUGHH-I SHOULD CLOSE-BLUGHH-THE WIN-BLUGHH-WINDOW!!' Phoenix closed the window as fast as she could.

SLAM!

'Oh, that was crazy.' Phoenix heaved a big sigh.

'Never open the window because we are going at 120,000 mph' Rigel commanded.

'What? Are we really going at 120,000 mph? Our speed record is only 13,000 mph.' Phoenix was flabbergasted.

'That is why Harita said that she could help us catch the door' Sagittarius guessed.

'You have arrived at your destination' Harita said.

'Where do we go out from? The door is mysteriously gone.' Auriga looked around the room.

'Sorry, the door has moved' Harita apologised.

'What? This room's door has moved?' Auriga was aghast.

'No, the magic door that you were trying to capture' Harita replied.

'Oh, *that* door.' Auriga exhaled.

'It says here that the door is 96,000 miles away from us' Rigel interrupted.

'Then we will be there in less than an hour' Sagittarius also interrupted.

'Now we are doing maths, aren't we?' Phoenix crossed her arms.

Everyone went silent, even the map. Phoenix could do some real damage. She hates maths, even just doing a small calculation.

A few minutes later …

'Sorry' Auriga finally said.

Phoenix did not reply. She just glared dangerously.

'I forgive you but ... You know, don't do that again.' Phoenix shrugged.

'Yes.' Rigel shuddered.

Auriga then looked at the window. everything was darkening to brownish red blur.

'*Speed increasing, increasing!*' Harita warned the team.

Auriga looked at the screen now, and the speed had somehow reduced to 120 mph. She also saw pale red floating ghosts around them. Auriga looked back at the window panicking: She saw ghost-like figures flying towards the forest.

'Look!' Auriga pointed to the window and the screen.

'This is devil strange.' Phoenix calmly said but with a slight panic in her voice.

'*Ghosts are surrounding us*' Harita warned them again.

'What is happening?' Cygnus put his hands on his head.

'Everyone calm down!' Phoenix said.

'*No time, the ghosts are going to shoot hayalet lightning!*' Harita said.

'What is hay'- 'Cygnus got cut off.

'*Evacuate, evacuate!*' Harita commanded.

Everyone ran to the door appearing in the wall, opened it, and ran outside before Harita turned into a map. The team saw the red body of the floating ghosts, their brownish-purple heads, pale black teeth, invisible mouths outlined by glowing green teeth, and pairs of white eyes.

The ghosts barely missed the team with a lightning-like shape charge. It smashed into the wall only nine inches away from the team.

The team and the map all ran away from the deadly ghosts.

'What the heck was that?' Phoenix breathed hard, half- choking on the cold air.

'That was …' Cygnus gasped '…a nightmare' he continued, throwing a stick at the ghost. But the stick melted in front of the glowing red creature.

The team then ran in the direction of the magic door.

Half an hour later …

'Oh, finally we are here.' Phoenix stopped in front of the magic door.

'We have to open the door quickly before it flies away' Cygnus said.

However, before anybody could open the door, it turned into a deadly green ghost. One of the other deadly creatures reached out one of his translucent hands before it turned into one massive palm and grabbed all of the team, Sagittarius, Auriga, Cygnus, and Phoenix, only missing Rigel and the hovering map.

Sagittarius, Auriga, Cygnus, and Phoenix instantly disappeared into the closing ghost-hand.

Harita and Rigel ran in the opposite direction. But another team of ghosts block the only way out.

'We are trapped.' Rigel ran back and forth.

' తలుపు ఇక్కడకు రండి! తలుపు ఇక్కడకు రండి! తలుపు ఇక్కడకు రండి! ''Harita said mysteriously.

Suddenly, a door appeared out of nowhere with bright light pouring from it.

That door had some holy spirits hidden behind it, so the ghosts were in danger. They immediately started to shriek in a weird language.

'*Cuideachadh, spiorad taibhse! cuideachadh, spiorad taibhse!*'[1] the ghosts said.

The ghosts were then being pulled back away from the door and started to disappear into thin air. It was as if an invisible vacuum cleaner were sucking them up whole. All the ghosts disappeared in less than a minute.

---

[1] Help, ghost spirit!

'What did you do?' Rigel looked around.

'నేను పరిశుద్ధాత్మ చేసాను' Harita said.

'Sorry, I mean, I called the holy spirits.' Harita translated.

'Wow ...' The boy was amazed.

Around Rigel and Harita, the dark forest started brightening till it was light orange. Rigel soon realised that the door was the magic door.

'That is the door we were looking for?' The boy sounded as if he didn't believe it as he pointed at the door before it disappeared.

'No, that is a holy clone' Harita explained.

'What is a holy'- 'Rigel got cut off.

'No time to explain!' Harita hovered in the air, moving backwards. *'There will be*

a big blast, a dangerous blast' Harita continued.

A colourful fire -- red, carmine, orange, yellow, yellow-green, green, blue, violet, purple, and white -- appeared out of nowhere.

After the fire stopped, Sagittarius, Phoenix, Cygnus, and Auriga appeared lying down with closed eyes.

'We have to help them.' Harita morphed into a hand, touching the team. All the colours mysteriously popped out from Harita's hand. The colours spread around their bodies.

'I am doing mustion healing' Harita said to Rigel.

The boy was half shocked, half curious.

One minute later…

Sagittarius, Phoenix, Cygnus, and Auriga opened their eyes.

'We are alive.' Auriga checked her body all over.

The team stood up.

'Thank you.' Phoenix thanked Rigel and the map.

'*It is all right.*' Harita morphed back into the hovering map.

'We have to capture that fast door.' Phoenix clasped her hands together.

Out of nowhere, the magic door appeared mysteriously.

'Turns out we don't need to catch that door.' Auriga shrugged.

'That isn't the clone, right?' Rigel asked Harita.

'*No.*' Harita identified the door.

'Let's go inside' Cygnus said.

The team walked up to the door and opened it. They stepped into some blue mist. They walked in further and further.

And then something mysterious happened.

***

Do you think that the door is where Lyra is trapped, or it is it a fake?

Where do you think the ghosts came from?

What do you think hayalet lighning is?

Is the headmaster a monster? If he is a monster, where is the real headmaster ?

Will the team survive or die?

Will Rigel be a saver soon?

And does Rigel save his parents? If he does, how does he do it?

Those questions will be answered in the next series of RIGEL

END

***

Printed in Great Britain
by Amazon

56973582R00081